the GARFIELD show

WITHDRAWN

PAPERCUTZ™

GRAPHIC NOVELS AVAILABLE FROM **PAPERCUT**Z ™

#6 "APPRENTICE SORCERER"

BASED ON THE ORIGINAL CHARACTERS CREATED BY
JIM DAVIS

PAPERCUT Z ™

NEW YORK

THE GARFIELD SHOW #6 "APPRENTICE SORCERER"

"THE GARFIELD SHOW" SERIES © 2016- DARGAUD MEDIA. ALL RIGHTS RESERVED.
© PAWS. "GARFIELD" & GARFIELD CHARACTERS TM & © PAWS INC. - ALL
RIGHTS RESERVED. THE GARFIELD SHOW—A DARGAUD MEDIA PRODUCTION.
IN ASSOCIATION WITH FRANCE3 WITH THE PARTICIPATION OF CENTRE NATIONAL
DE LA CINÉMATOGRAPHIE AND THE SUPPORT OF REGION ILE-DE-FRANCE.
A SERIES DEVELOPED BY PHILIPPE VIDAL, ROBERT REA AND STEVE BALISSAT.
BASED UPON THE CHARACTERS CREATED BY JIM DAVIS. ORIGINAL STORIES:
"STINK, STANK, STUNK," "BARKING MAD," AND "APPRENTICE SORCERER"
(ORIGINALLY "BEWITCHED") WRITTEN BY JULIEN MAGNAT; "BULLDOG OF DOOM"
WRITTEN BY SAMUEL BARKSDALE.

CEDRIC MICHIELS - COMICS ADAPTATION
JOE JOHNSON - TRANSLATIONS
TONY ISABELLA - DIALOGUE RESTORATION
TOM ORZECHOWSKI - LETTERING
JEFF WHITMAN - PRODUCTION COORDINATOR
BETHANY BRYAN - ASSOCIATE EDITOR
JIM SALICRUP
EDITOR-IN-CHIEF

ISBN: 978-1-62991-449-7 PAPERBACK EDITION
ISBN: 978-1-62991-450-3 HARDCOVER EDITION

PRINTED IN CHINA
FEBRUARY 2016 BY TOPPAN LEEFUNG PRINTING LIMITED
JIN JU GUAN LI QU,
DA LING SHAN TOWN,
DONGGUAN, PRC
CHINA

PAPERCUTZ BOOKS MAY BE PURCHASED FOR BUSINESS OR PROMOTIONAL USE. FOR INFORMATION ON
BULK PURCHASES PLEASE CONTACT MACMILLAN CORPORATE AND PREMIUM SALES DEPARTMENT AT
(800) 221-7945 X5442.

DISTRIBUTED BY MACMILLAN
FIRST PAPERCUTZ PRINTING

STINK, STANK, STUNK

NOT CUTE. DEFINITELY NOT CUTE. ABOUT AS **NOT** CUTE AS YOU CAN GET.

HOW DID **THEY** MAKE THE "CUTEST PET PAGEANT" FINALS?

NERMAL...

...REMIND ME HOW MUCH **LONGER** YOU'RE PLANNING TO OVERSTAY YOUR WELCOME.

THE PAGEANT FINALS ARE **TONIGHT** AT THE TOWN HALL.

I'M GOING TO **WIN**, OF COURSE.

PSHHHHH

PSHHHHH

I LOOK GREAT AND ⇒*SNIFF*⇐ I SMELL GREAT!

IN OTHER NEWS... A **SKUNK** WAS SPOTTED DOWNTOWN--

--PROMPTING THE POLICE TO **LOCK DOWN** THE AREA.

⇒EWW!⇐ I **HATE** SKUNKS.

SKUNKS ARE MAMMALS WHO CAN CREATE A TERRIBLE **ODOR.**

YUCK! ODIE, WHAT IS THAT ⋛ SNIFF SNIFF ⋚ AWFUL SMELL?

THAT WOULD BE MOI...

⋛ ULP! ⋚ IT'S A... IT'S A... IT'S A...

SKUNK!

YAAAAAH!

NOooooo!

THAT WAS SO GOOD...

...I WISH I COULD WATCH IT AGAIN IN SLOW MOTION.

I'M TAKING MY REPULSIVE NEW POWERS OUT FOR A STROLL.

AH, THE TWO MEANEST DOGS IN THE HOOD.

HELLO, BOYS...

⋛ ULK?! ⋚

⋛ ILK?! ⋚

IT GOT AWAY!

DARN. IF THIS WERE THE CARTOON AND NOT THE COMIC BOOK...

...WE'D BE GETTING SOME JAZZY CHASE MUSIC RIGHT NOW.

WHERE IS IT?

IT CAN'T BE FAR!

I NEED TO FIND SOME COVER, QUICK.

I CAN LOSE THEM IN THE PARK.

⇒WHEW!⇐

⇒PSSST!⇐ OVER HERE!

?

THEY'RE GONE. THE COAST IS CLEAR.

THANKS. YOU SAVED ME.

AT FIRST, IT WAS KINDA FUN TO SCARE PEOPLE, BUT THAT GOT OLD PRETTY FAST.

I HAVE TO ASK... ISN'T IT A BIT, UM, *LONELY* TO BE A SKUNK?

OH, IT'S ALL RIGHT...

WE SKUNKS ARE PRETTY SOLITARY CREATURES ANYWAY. WE *LIKE* TRANQUILITY.

BUT THIS IS *ONE* THING I'VE ALWAYS DREAMT OF DOING.

IT'S SILLY, BUT I ALWAYS WANTED TO BE IN A PAGEANT. JUST ONCE BE KNOWN FOR SOMETHING OTHER THAN MY ODOR.

HMMM...

IF YOU HELP ME GET THIS PAINT AND SMELL OFF...

I THINK I CAN...

...MAKE YOUR DREAM COME *TRUE.*

MY FRIENDS, I AM STILL EDDIE GOURMAND, YOUR **HOST**, AND HERE'S WHAT YOU'VE BEEN WAITING FOR SINCE THIS AWARDS SHOW BEGAN THREE **HOURS** AGO.

JUST IMAGINE IF THESE BELOVED PETS COULD HAVE GIVEN **SPEECHES.**

HERE ARE THE **FINALISTS** IN THIS YEAR'S CUTEST PET COMPETITION!

JUST GET **ON** WITH IT AND GIVE ME THE TROPHY ALREADY!

I'LL ANNOUNCE THE WINNER... RIGHT AFTER THIS **COMMERCIAL**.

SUPER! I GUESS I COULD FRESHEN UP AGAIN.

THE DRESSING ROOM...

THERE'S NERMAL'S PERFUME...

WITH A MIRROR IN THE ROOM...

ZIP

...HE WON'T EVEN **NOTICE** THE SWITCH.

JUST A QUICK SPLASH OF PERFUME AND THEN I'LL PICK UP MY TROPHY.

AHHH...

HMM... IT SORT OF ⸫WHIFF⸫ SMELLS IN HERE. NEXT TIME...

...I'LL INSIST ON A *PRIVATE* DRESSING ROOM.

IN A MOMENT, I'LL OPEN THE JUDGES' ENVELOPE AND REVEAL WHICH PET IS THE CUTEST OF THE *CUTE!*

IT STINKS IN HERE! I FEEL FAINT...

THE ⸫CHOKE⸫ WINNER IS NOT...

...*THIS SMELLY CAT!*

GET ME A *GAS MASK!*

WHAT?!

GET IT OUT OF HERE AND CALL THE *EPA!*

NO! I'M THE *WINNER!* I'M *ALWAYS* THE WINNER!

WHAT PART OF *"WORLD'S CUTEST KITTEN"* DON'T YOU GET?

I DEMAND A *RECOUNT!*

POOR NERMAL...

NOW IT'S YOUR TURN!

the GARFIELD show

THE BULLDOG OF DOOM

THIS IS THE STORY OF THE PIE, THE CAT AND THE BULLDOG OF DOOM...

IT BEGINS WITH A NEWLY-BAKED *PIE* WHOSE AROMA DRIFTS TO SURROUNDING HOMES...

...AND SOON TO THE NOSTRILS OF *THIS* CAT...

THAT BULLY *BRUNO* IS ON THE PROWL.

UH-OH.

HE'S DECIDED TO HELP HIMSELF TO THAT OLD MAN'S LUNCH.

EVEN I WOULDN'T DO SOMETHING *THAT* ROTTEN.

BRUNO! WHAT YOU DOING *HERE?* WHY AREN'T YOU OVER ON *CRESTVIEW?*

HUH?

WHAT'S HAPPENING ON *CRESTVIEW?*

THE AROMA SPOKE TO THE CAT AND IT SAID "DON'T I SMELL DELICIOUS?"

I THINK I LOVE YOU, PIE.

THEN AGAIN, I LOVE ALL PIES.

EXCEPT FOR *RAISIN* PIES.

THOSE TASTE LIKE SOGGY GRAVEL.

UNFORTUNATELY, THE WONDROUS PIE WAS NOT *ALONE*...

OH, NO. IT'S HIM...

...THE *BULLDOG OF DOOM!*

GRRRR

THE PIE AND I CAN NEVER BE...

NO! I CAN'T LEAVE THAT DELICIOUS-SMELLING...

...WHATEVER-KIND-OF-PIE-IT-IS...

...SIT THERE UNEATEN. I MUST BRAVE THE BEAST.

GARFIELD!

GRRR... THERE WERE NO FREE *PANCAKES* ON CRESTVIEW AVENUE.

YOU *TRICKED* ME!

THAT WAS WHEN THE CAT HAD WHAT SEEMED LIKE A GOOD IDEA...

BUT CAN'T YOU SMELL THAT DELICIOUS *PIE?*

LET ME EXPLAIN...

PIE? OH, NO! THIS IS AN-OTHER TRICK!

I DON'T KNOW WHAT KIND OF PIE.

BUT, HEY, IT'S PIE.

I *CAN* SMELL IT!

I LOVE PIE EVEN MORE THAN BEATING UP ON *YOU!*

I WAS THINKING WE COULD *SPLIT* THE PIE...

DREAM ON, TUBBY. THAT WHATEVER-IT-IS-PIE IS MINE.

ALL MINE!

HE'S IN THE LAST CAGE ON THE RIGHT, MISTER ARBUCKLE!

THANKS FOR CALLING ME, AL. I WAS STARTING TO GET WORRIED.

YOU'RE PROBABLY WONDERING HOW I ENDED UP *HERE*, RIGHT?

OH, HI.

I'LL TELL YOU THE WHOLE STORY.

PRETEND YOU JUST HIT *"REWIND"* ON THE REMOTE.

THE BEST, MOST HUMANE WAY TO TEACH YOUR DOG BARKING *ISN'T* OKAY.

WOOF WOOF!

BEEP

BAD DOGGY. BAD DOGGY. NO BARKING ALLOWED.

≋ WHINE ≋

COMES WITH THREE LEVELS OF TRAINING AND A LOCK-IN SAFETY LATCH.

ORDER NOW!

ONE SIZE FITS ALL. DOG NOT INCLUDED. CLICK HERE TO ORDER WITH SPECIAL ULTRA-SUPER SPEEDY SHIPPING!

I'M CLICKING! I'M CLICKING!

TOOT TOOT

ZIPPPPPPPP

WONDER WHAT *TOOK* THEM SO LONG.

BEHOLD... THE END TO BARKING.

26

I'LL JUST PUT THIS ON ODIE AND...

...AND THE LATCH WON'T OPEN.

NOTHING IN THE MANUAL ABOUT HOW TO REMOVE THIS. NOTHING? YOU'VE *GOT* TO BE KIDDING ME.

≈GRRR!≈ OPEN UP, YOU STATE-OF-THE-ART HUNK OF *JUNK!*

GRRRRR

WOOF?

BAD DOGGY. BAD DOGGY. NO BARKING ALLOWED.

JUST STAY CALM. JON WILL FIND A WAY TO REMOVE THIS WHEN HE COMES HOME IN...

...SIX HOURS. SIX LONG AND SEEMINGLY ENDLESS HOURS.

"I THOUGHT I COULD JUST *SLEEP* UNTIL JON CAME HOME.

ZZZZZZZ
ZZZZZZZ
ZZZZZZ

"SLEEP IS, AFTER ALL, MY DEFAULT SETTING.

"BEING WRONG WAS GETTING TO BE A BAD HABIT...

WOOF!

WOOF!

BEEP BEEP BEEP

WOOF!

BAD DOGGY. BAD DOGGY. NO BARKING ALLOWED.

GRIND

BAD DOGGY! DIDN'T YOU HEAR ME?

NO BARKING ALLOWED!

I'VE GOT TO GET THIS COLLAR OFF ME!

I NEED TOOLS!

THERE ARE *TOO* MANY DOGS IN THIS NEIGHBORHOOD.

I *CAN'T* WAIT UNTIL JON GETS HOME.

GNN!

ARRGH! IT'S NO USE.

IT'S TOO STRONG.

CONGRATULATIONS. YOU HAVE SUCCESSFULLY ACTIVATED *LEVEL TWO* OF THE REINFORCE-MENT TRAINING SOFTWARE.

LEVEL *TWO?* THIS CAN'T *POSSIBLY* BE GOOD.

28

"...UNTIL I WOKE UP HERE AND STARTED THE LONGEST FLASH-BACK IN THE HISTORY OF THIS PAPERCUTZ GRAPHIC NOVEL."

THIS IS A REALLY STRANGE COLLAR.

YES! GET IT OFF ME! I'LL DO ANYTHING YOU ASK! I'LL EVEN CUT MY LASAGNA CONSUMP-TION TO NINE A DAY!

LET'S SEE HOW THIS COMES OFF...

OH, IT JUST POPS OPEN WHEN YOU TOUCH THIS BUTTON...

THAT'S IT? THAT'S ALL IT TAKES?

HMM... SO YOU PUT IT ON LIKE THIS...

IT'S A TIGHT FIT.

THIS IS LIKE DEJA VU ALL OVER AGAIN.

IT SHOULD JUST COME OFF WITH A SECOND TOUCH OF THE BUTTON.

THIS IS TOO PAINFUL TO WATCH.

I'M GETTING OUT OF HERE

HEY, NOT **THAT** DOOR, CAT!

THAT'S THE DOG POUND IN THERE!

YOU JUST PUSH THIS BUTTON...

OH, NO! YOU'VE LET THE DOGS OUT!

NOT SENSING ANY GRATITUDE FROM THEM.

JUST PUSH...

WOOF!

BARK!

BARK!

YOU DON'T GET THE NO BARKING THING, DO YOU?

AD DOGGY! BAD DOGGY!

VZZZZZAP

AAAAAAH!

HOW COULD ANYTHING FROM THE **INTERNET** CAUSE SO MUCH TROUBLE? I WONDER IF I COULD JUST ORDER SOME **EARPLUGS**.

NOT AGAIN!

BARK BARK!

THIS IS THE WORST ENDING IN THE UNIVERSE.

WOOF WOOF WOOF!

THE END

WATCH OUT FOR PAPERCUTZ

Welcome to the not-even-slightly stinky but altogether spooky sixth THE GARFIELD SHOW graphic novel from Papercutz, the only slightly scary boys and ghouls devoted to publishing great graphic novels for all ages. I'm Jim Salicrup, Editor-in-Chief and sometimes a somewhat stinky (from spending way too much time at his desk) skunk, here to talk about various things that come to mind after enjoying this particular volume of THE GARFIELD SHOW.

Speaking of which (not witch), for those of you who pay far too much attention and are wondering why this book's title is "Apprentice Sorcerer," instead of "Stink, Stank, Stunk," let's just say we changed our mind. If you look at page two of the first printing of THE GARFIELD SHOW #5 "Fido Food Feline," you'll see that we were indeed planning to call this volume "Stink, Stank, Stunk," but when we saw the artwork for the "Apprentice Sorcerer," we realized that would stand out from all our previous covers, in a really nice way. We hope you agree. (That, and at 30 pages, it takes up almost half of this graphic novel!)

Speaking of witches (not which), it seems Papercutz is now attracting almost as many witches as we are cats! One of our newest hits is an original graphic novel by Deb Lucke entitled "The Lunch Witch." Such an intriguing title may prompt you to ask, "What's it about?" We'll resist the very strong temptation to say "about 176 pages," and instead actually answer the question, by telling you exactly what it says on THE LUNCH WITCH page on Papercutz.com…

…For generations and generations, the women of Grunhilda's (She's the Lunch Witch!) family have stirred up trouble in a big, black pot. Grunhilda inherits her famous ancestors' recipes and cauldron, but no one believes in magic anymore. Despite the fact that Grunhilda's only useful skill is cooking up pots full of foul brew, she finds a job listing that might suit her: school lunch lady. She delights in scaring the

kids until she meets Madison, a girl with thick glas and unfinished homework who doesn't fit in. The outsiders recognize each other. Madison needs hel school and at home, but helping people goes again everything Grunhilda's believes in as a witch! Will girl be able to thaw the Lunch Witch's icy heart? O will Grunhilda turn her back on a kindred spirit?

The Lunch Witch Copyright © 2016 by Deb

And that's the premise of the first volume of th all-new THE LUNCH WITCH graphic novel series from Papercutz. The critics have raved about THE LUNCH WITCH, and we're already publishing a second printing of the first volume to help meet demand. We suspect Abigail Cauldron would get along well with Grunhilda's frenemy Madison. An we strongly suspect that if you enjoyed "Apprentic Sorcerer," you'll enjoy THE LUNCH WITCH. You'l find THE LUNCH WITCH lurking at your favorite booksellers, probably somewhere near all THE GARFIELD SHOW graphic novels. Guess there's ju something about cats and witches that just seems go together!

Thanks, JIM

STAY IN TOUCH!

EMAIL: SALICRUP@PAPERCUTZ.COM
WEB: PAPERCUTZ.COM
TWITTER: @PAPERCUTZGN
FACEBOOK: PAPERCUTZGRAPHICNOVELS
BIRTHDAY CARDS: PAPERCUTZ, 160 BROADWAY,
SUITE 700, EAST WING, NEW
YORK, NY 10038

THE HEARTLESS WITCH SEARCHED FOR *THREE* LEGENDARY MAGICAL ARTIFACTS SACRED TO OUR KIND...

BY *COMBINING* THEIR POWERS, VARICELLA COULD CAST THE *FORBIDDEN SPELL OF THE MOON*...

YOU MEAN--?

YES, THEY WERE THE *QUICKSILVER SLIPPERS*, THE *BROOM OF SORROWS*, AND THE *WAND OF BITTERNESS*.

"...AND TRANSFORMING ALL HUMANS INTO HELP-LESS *TOADS!*

"...PLUNGING THE ENTIRE *WORLD* INTO ETERNAL DARKNESS...

"VARICELLA *HAD* TO BE STOPPED BEFORE SHE CAST THE SPELL.

"...BANISHING VARICELLA INTO THE PAGES OF A *MAGIC SPELL BOOK!*"

"THE OTHER WITCHES UNITED AS *ONE*...

NAAAAAAAAH

CLAM

THE MAGICAL ARTIFACTS WERE **SCATTERED** ACROSS THE MAGIC REALM SO NO ONE COULD EVER BRING THEM **TOGETHER** AGAIN.

FOR THERE ARE GOOD **AND** BAD WITCHES... AND WE MUST ALWAYS BE READY TO PROTECT HUMANITY FROM THE BAD ONES.

AUNTIE, CAN VARICELLA EVER **ESCAPE** FROM THE ENCHANTED BOOK?

FOR EVERY SPELL, THERE IS A **COUNTER** SPELL. THAT IS WHY WE GUARD THE BOOK.

...AND THAT IS WHY YOU STUDY YOUR WITCHCRAFT.

NOW OFF TO SCHOOL WITH YOU.

I **WILL** STUDY HARD... AND BECOME THE MOST POWERFUL GOOD WITCH **EVER!**

!

KEEEEE

KEEEEE

DON'T WORRY, **BRUCE.** YOU'RE MY **FAMILIAR.** I'LL TAKE YOU WITH ME **WHEREVER** I GO! YOU, ME AND MY **WAND!**

OOPS!

KAZAPP

OH, MY GOSH! I DIDN'T HAVE THE *SAFETY* ON!

VOOP

BRUCE?

SQEEE

KEEEE
KEEE

KEEEEE

BRUCE! COME BACK!

IT WAS AN *ACCIDENT!* I DIDN'T MEAN TO *FRIGHTEN* YOU!

OH, MY...

I HAVE TO CATCH HIM!

IF I GO TO WITCH CLASS WITHOUT MY FAMILIAR, I'LL GET AN *"F"*!

PLEASE DON'T FLY AWAY! YOU'RE MY BEST *FRIEND!*

I'LL GIVE YOU *TREATS..*

PICK UP THE PACE, ODIE. THAT NEW PIZZA AT VITO'S WON'T EAT ITSELF.

WOOF!

WOOF?

KEEEEEE

HE'S FLYING TOO FAST!

SWOOP

PIE?

SAY, WOULD YOU DO A FAVOR FOR A NEIGHBOR?

YOU WOULD?

WOOF?

ZIMBALOO BODOBOU!

⇥EEP⇤

NEVER SAW THAT COMING.

HOW CUTE!

YOU'RE PERFECT! NOBODY WILL SPOT THE DIFFERENCE!

ALL WE NEED NOW IS YOUR CAGE.

ABIGAIL IS A WITCH...

...AND ODIE IS A BAT.

I HATE MONDAYS.

ABIGAIL! IT'S TIME TO LEAVE FOR SCHOOL!

ME AND... UH... **BRUCE** ARE READY TO GO!

WITCH, BAT, MONDAY, NO PIZZA...

I HATE THIS STORY SO FAR.

≥HUFF≤

≥PUFF≤

≥HUFF≤

THAT BOOK ≥GIGGLE≤ GETS GREAT MILEAGE.

TRANSPORTUS SCOTTYUS!

BYE BYE, AUNTIE!

LISTEN TO COUSIN **WINONA.** SHE'S YOUR **TEACHER** NOW.

≥ULP≤

THEY VANISHED INTO THAT **GLOW.**

I THINK I'LL BAKE SOME FROG MUFFINS.

FROG MUFFINS? THAT SOUNDS WORSE THAN RAISIN PIE.

THAT BOOK CAN FIND ODIE AND CHANGE HIM BACK TO HIS USUAL SLOBBERING SELF.

ODIE?

WOOF!

I'LL GET YOU OUT OF THERE.

HEE HEE HEE HEE HEE

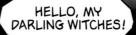

HELLO, MY DARLING WITCHES!

HELLO, MISS WINONA!

I HAVE A BAD FEELING...

...ABOUT THIS.

TODAY, WE HAVE A SURPRISE *QUIZ.*

FIRST, YOU WILL USE YOUR WAND TO RETRIEVE YOUR FAMILIAR...

...AND THEN TURN THEM INTO A *TEACUP!*

DON'T YOU *DARE* HARM HER!

POW

≈URKK!≈

PUNT

SPLAT

THIS IS WHERE WE START RUNNING AGAIN.

JUST ONE SECOND...

SOMEHOW WE'VE GOT TO *STOP* VARICELLA ...

...AND THIS BOOK MAY BE OUR ONLY *HOPE!*

GRRRR... I'LL GET YOU, ABIGAIL!

AND YOUR LITTLE CAT AND DOG, TOO!

THIS IS WHAT HAPPENS WHEN YOU SPEND A THOUSAND YEARS...

...TRAPPED INSIDE A MOLDY OLD BOOK!

SINCE WE'RE NOT ALL MUNCHING ON FLIES-- SORRY, NONA-- I THINK WE'VE LOST HER.

SHE DOESN'T SEEM LIKE THE FORGIVING TYPE.

IN THE *STORY*, VARICELLA NEEDED THREE MAGICAL ITEMS FOR HER SPELL TO BRING ON THE ETERNAL DARKNESS AND TURN ALL HUMANS INTO *FROGS*.

THERE'S THE *BROOM OF SORROWS*.

IT CAN TAKE US ANYWHERE.

THE *QUICK-SILVER SLIPPERS* TO BECOME INVISIBLE.

AND THE *WAND OF BITTERNESS*.

IT'S THE MOST *POWERFUL* WAND IN THE REALM.

WE HAVE TO FIND THEM BEFORE VARICELLA GETS HER GRUBBY GREEN HANDS ON THEM.

THIS MAP IN THE BOOK SHOWS THEIR *LOCATIONS*.

THE BROOM OF SORROWS IS THE *CLOSEST*.

THERE'S NO TIME TO WASTE. LET'S HOP TO IT.

RUNNING AND NOW HOPPING.

I HATE THESE LONG STORIES.

"STRONGER THAN THE WAND." WHAT WAS THAT THING MRS. CAULDRON SAID BEFORE SHE BECAME A STATUE?

THE STRONGEST MAGIC DOESN'T COME FROM A WAND, BUT FROM A HEART!

THE PENDANT THAT AUNTIE WORE!

WHERE IS IT?

WOOF! WOOOOF!

OH, ODIE! YOU'VE BEEN *GUARDING* IT ALL THIS TIME!

VARICELLA! IT'S YOU AND *ME!*

I'M TALKING TO *YOU,* AUNTIE VARICELLA!

IT'S TIME TO *PRUNE* THE FAMILY TREE!

YOU DARE?!